SOUTH HOLLAND PUBLIC LIBRARY

3 1350 00305 1960

W9-CCG-137

**South Holland Public Library**
South Holland, Illinois

DISCARD

GAYLORD

# Wodney Wat's Wobot

Text copyright © 2011 by Helen Lester
Illustrations copyright © 2011 by Lynn Munsinger

All rights reserved. For information about permission to reproduce
selections from this book, write to Permissions,
Houghton Mifflin Harcourt Publishing Company,
215 Park Avenue South, New York, New York 10003.

Houghton Mifflin Books for Children is an imprint of
Houghton Mifflin Harcourt Publishing Company.

www.hmhbooks.com

The text of this book is set in Garamond.

*Library of Congress Cataloging-in-Publication Data*
Lester, Helen.
Wodney Wat's wobot / written by Helen Lester ; illustrated by Lynn Munsinger.
p. cm.
Summary: When Wodney Wat, who cannot pronounce the letter R,
gets a talking robot for his birthday, it turns out to be more than just a fun gift.
ISBN 978-0-547-36756-9
[1. Robots—Fiction. 2. Speech disorders—Fiction. 3. Schools—Fiction.
4. Rodents—Fiction.] I. Munsinger, Lynn, ill. II. Title.
PZ7.L56285Wo 2011
[E]—dc22
2010044363

3 1350 00305 1960
DISCARD

Manufactured in China
LEO 10 9 8 7 6 5 4 3 2 1

4500305118

# Wodney Wat's Wobot

Written by Helen Lester
Illustrated by Lynn Munsinger

Houghton Mifflin Books for Children
Houghton Mifflin Harcourt
BOSTON  NEW YORK  2011

It was Wodney Wat's birthday.
His real name was Rodney Rat, but he couldn't pronounce his *r*'s.

But never mind. Wodney had just unwrapped something.

"What a tewiffic pwesent! Thank you! What is it?"

His friends hopped up and down in excitement.
"It's a robot! It's a robot!"
"See that button on its nose?" asked Grizzlefriz Guinea Pig.

"Push it and whisper 'pickle,'" suggested Minifeet Mouse.

Wodney pushed the button and whispered, "Pickle."
**PICKLE . . .** said the robot.
Hairy Hamster hiccupped. "Now," he said, "try 'Having the hiccups is very annoying.'"

Wodney pushed the button and whispered, "Having the hiccups is vewy annoying."
**HAVING . . . THE . . . HICCUPS . . . IS . . .
VERY . . . ANNOYING . . .** said the robot.

"I think it even helps me pwonounce my *awwwww's*," squealed Wodney.

"What a gweat contwaption! A talking wobot!"

Everyone wanted to try it!
WOW, was it fun!

In the cafeteria he whispered, "May I please have some wibs and wice?"
MAY . . . I . . . PLEASE . . . HAVE . . . SOME . . .
RIBS . . . AND . . . RICE . . .

At gym time he whispered, "Will you please waise me up to the wings?"
WILL . . . YOU . . . PLEASE . . . RAISE . . .
ME . . . UP . . . TO . . . THE . . . RINGS . . .
And when Miss Fuzzleworth asked Wodney the sum of 2 plus 1,
he whispered, "Thwee."
THREE . . . said the robot.

"I'm having a bawwel of fun!" giggled Wodney.
A barrel of fun . . . until one morning.

"HOWDY, PARDNERS! I'M BAAAAACK," thundered Camilla Capybara
as she burst into the classroom.
Teeth rattled, whiskers twitched, and eyes stared in disbelief.

Everyone thought Camilla had gone west. Forever.

"You don't look any smarter."
She thumped Grizzlefriz and Hairy
on the head.

"You're sure not any bigger." She lifted Minifeet and Wodney up by the collar.

"AND," she added, sweeping pencils and papers off Miss Fuzzleworth's desk and plunking herself down, "I'm still the World's Meanest Rodent. So there."

Miss Fuzzleworth said in a trembling voice, "Camilla, dear, we thought you had gone west."

"And I've got the hat and the top-of-the-line boots to prove it!" bellowed Camilla. "I went west, and kept going west and kept going west and kept going west *alllllll* the way around the world until . . . here I am. You'd better believe it."

They believed it.

So the rattled rodents and twitching teacher had to live with Camilla and all her shenanigans.

Until one day.
It was quiz time.

"Minifeet," asked Miss Fuzzleworth, "how many eggs are in a dozen?"

"Twelve," replied Minifeet.

"Even a *baaaaayby* knows THAT," snorted Camilla.

Miss Fuzzleworth continued, "Grizzlefriz, what is the largest member of the rodent species?"

"The capybara," answered Grizzlefriz.

"*Alllllllll right!*" boomed Camilla, flexing her muscles.

Now it was Wodney's turn.

"What is the shape of the world?" Wodney pushed his robot's button and whispered, "Wound."

R . . . R . . . R . . . R . . . R . . .

"Shape of the World?" repeated Miss Fuzzleworth.

"Wound," Wodney said in a louder voice.

R . . . R . . . R . . . R . . . R . . .

"Something's wong with my wobot," squeaked Wodney, pushing the nose button again.

Camilla danced around the room chanting.

*Nananana na na*
*Someone's got a stut-ter*
*R-r-r-r-r*
*Someone's got a stut-ter*

Then the R . . . R . . . R . . . changed to
**RRRRRRRR.**
Whoa. Camilla stopped dancing.
If there was one thing that frightened her, it was
growly things.
Things that went **RRRRRRRR.**
Like tigers. She hid under a desk.

Or grizzly bears. She hopped up on the windowsill.
Or lions. Now she was behind the bookcase.

RRRRRRRRRRRRRRRRRRRRRRRRᴿᴿ . . . And then the robot was silent.

Nothing. Not a peep.

"Something's wong, vewwy wong, tewwibly wong with my wobot. I think it has cwoaked." A big tear fell on Wodney's foot.

Feeling safe in the silence, Camilla stomped out from behind the bookcase.

Her mean eyes scanned her classmates.

"Don't you know ANYthing?'
She whipped a gown out of her saddlebag and put it on.
"What a bunch of bozos."
*SNAP.* On went the rubber gloves.
"How clueless can you get?"
Now the surgical mask.
"All that robot needs is a new battery. DUH."

Reaching into the bottom of her bag, Camilla pulled out a battery.
"Picked this baby up in China," she announced.
*Kachung.* Out went the old.
*Kaching.* In went the new.

"Now try it, doofus."

"I'm gwateful," whispered Wodney.

I'M . . . GRATEFUL . . . said the robot.

"And I just might be leaving," stated Camilla.
"I'm much too smart for this class. I could go to high school
for my PhD, after all. But no. There ought to be SOME brains
in this place. You need me here. So there."

The only sound to be heard was the rattle of rodent teeth.

Then at that horrible moment, Wodney pushed the robot's nose button and whispered, "wwwwwwwwwwwwww."

RRRRRRRRRRRRR

# RRRRRRRR!

said the robot.

Camilla, who had been about to plunk herself back on Miss Fuzzleworth's desk, plunked down on the floor instead.

Wodney pushed the button again "Wwwwwwwwwww."

# RRRRRRRRR.

EXIT

Camilla rolled herself into a ball and RRRRRRRRRolled out the door.

Now everyone cheered.

"Hooway for Wodney Wat! Hooway for Wodney Wat's Wobot!"

And as for Wodney, he had a wonderful time playing with his robot,

but sometimes he gave it a west.

DISCARD